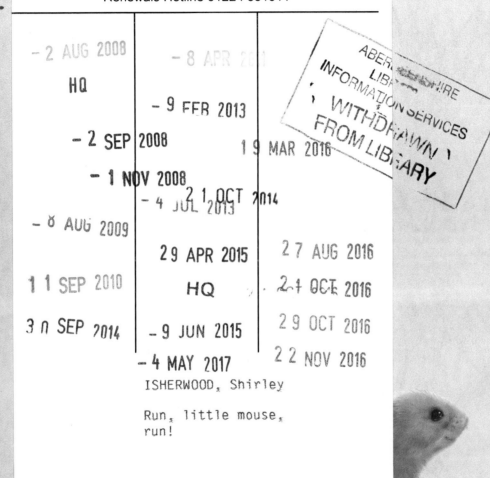

ISHERWOOD, Shirley

Run, little mouse,
run!

For Kia Whitehead
~ S I

For Lisa
~ S M

LITTLE TIGER PRESS
An imprint of Magi Publications
1 The Coda Centre, 189 Munster Road, London SW6 6AW
www.littletigerpress.com

First published in Great Britain 2008

Text copyright © Shirley Isherwood 2008
Illustrations copyright © Simon Mendez 2008
Shirley Isherwood and Simon Mendez have asserted their rights
to be identified as the author and illustrator of this work under
the Copyright, Designs and Patents Act, 1988

A CIP catalogue record for this book is available
from the British Library

Printed in Singapore

2 4 6 8 10 9 7 5 3 1

Run, Little Mouse, Run!

Shirley Isherwood

Simon Mendez

LITTLE TIGER PRESS

London

The field mouse was snuggled asleep in his
nest when a noise woke him up. He was puzzled.
Nothing normally woke him during the day –
he was a night animal and slept so soundly.

But the noise grew louder . . . and louder . . .
and louder. Something was coming towards him . . .

It was a big machine. Roaring through the field it went, cutting down the corn. Soon it would reach his nest. Nothing could stop it!

"Where should I go?" the field mouse cried. "This is my home!"

The field mouse ran. But he had never been out in the day, and the bright sun and the sky dazzled him. He did not know which way to turn.

Suddenly, a tiny patch of blue fluttered down from the sky. It was a butterfly.

"Go to the woods," she said. "There you will be safe."

So the field mouse ran through
the rustling stalks of corn.

When he reached a fence, he
slipped through – and then he
stopped, amazed. The meadow
was beautiful! Long grass waved
above him; yellow flowers
bent their heads.

"I could make my home here,"
thought the field mouse.
"I would be happy here."

But then he smelled a scent
that he knew too well . . .

It was the scent of his enemy. A tawny
fox was slinking through the grass.
The field mouse ran for his life.

Up ahead, he saw a hole in a wall, just big enough to hide him. Could he reach it before the fox pounced?

He scrambled in, just in time, and held his breath. Through a chink in the stones, he saw his enemy, sniffing this way and that. Then the fox turned and padded away.

The field mouse climbed to the top of the wall and looked out. There were the woods! And they were only a field away. Soon he would be safe.

Then he saw a family of baby rabbits. They looked
so happy, playing in the sun. They had long ears
and their noses twitched.

The field mouse crept closer until he was almost nose-to-nose with one of the rabbits. How lovely it was to make a new friend.

The daytime world is wonderful, he thought.

Suddenly, one of the rabbits thumped the ground
with his paws in warning. The rabbits all darted
off in a panic. The field mouse froze.

I am alone, he thought.
Alone and in danger.

Hovering above him was a hawk. The tall trees
of the woods seemed far, far away. There was
nowhere to hide. The field mouse must run
once more. It was the only thing left to do.
Above him was the beating of wings.
It was a sound that said, *This is the end
of things*.

The field mouse ran and ran towards the trees
and, at last, he was amongst them. The hawk
swooped down, then turned and flew away.

The field mouse watched him go. He stood,
catching his breath, happy to be alive,
but very, very tired.

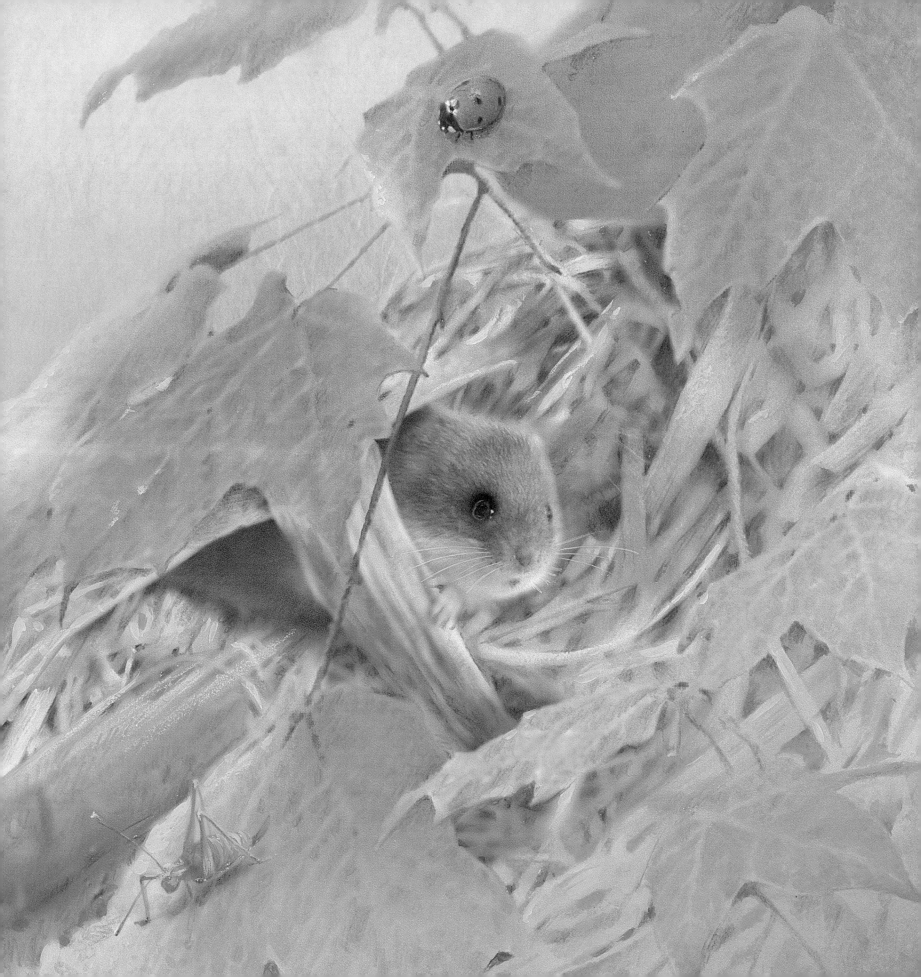

He crept under a little heap of fallen leaves. But there, right in front of him, was a sleepy-looking mouse!

"I'm sorry," said the field mouse. "I didn't know this was your nest."

But the sleepy mouse just said, "It's so nice to have a friend drop in," and went to sleep again!

So the field mouse lay down by the side of his new friend, in his new home, and fell fast asleep.